Too Many Emmas

An Ivy and Mack story

T0337070

Written by Juliet Clare Bell

Illustrated by Gustavo Mazali

with Szépvölgyi Eszter

Collins

Who and what is in this story?

Listen and say

Dad

Mack

Ivy

milkshake

Uncle Lee came to the door with Luke and Emma. They were Ivy and Mack's cousins.

"Let's go to the swimming pool," said Ivy.

"And after swimming, we always go to Claire's Café!" said Mack.

"It's got the best milkshakes!" said Dad.

"And a fantastic playground!" said Ivy.

The bus came and the children ran on.

Dad asked Emma about school.

"I like it but there are two more Emmas in my class!" said Emma.

"There's an Emma in my class, *too*," said Mack.

"*And* mine!" said Ivy.

"Yes! And there's an Emma in my class!" said Luke.

"The teacher calls us Emma One, Emma Two and Emma Three. I'm Emma Three," said Emma.

"There are *too many* Emmas!" laughed Luke.

"Don't worry, Emma," said Ivy. "Let's play a game. I spy with my little eye, something beginning with 'S'."

Emma said, "That's easy! Supermarket. Now me! I spy with my little eye, something beginning with 'B'."

"Bookshop!" said Ivy.

"I want to play, too," said Mack.

"You can!" said Ivy. "I spy with my little eye, something beginning with 'H'."

"I know! It's hospital!" said Mack. "Do you want to play, Luke?"

"No!" said Luke.

"Quick," said Dad. "Time to get off the bus! This is our stop."

"Can I ring the bell?" asked Mack.

"How fast can you swim, Ivy?" said Luke.

"Very fast," said Ivy.

"Yes, she can," said Mack to Luke. "And I can swim fast, too!"

Luke looked at Emma. "Where's your swimming bag, Emma?"

Emma's bag was on the bus.

Luke was angry. "There are places next to the pool to sit," Luke said, "Emma you sit with Dad and watch *us* swim."

"Now then, Luke! Be nice!" said Uncle Lee.

"Yes. Be nice, Luke!" said Ivy.

"But Dad ..." said Luke.

"We all make mistakes, Luke," said Ivy. "Let's do a different thing ..."

Emma was sad.

"I know!" said Mack. "We can go to Claire's Café, can't we Dad?"

They went to Claire's Café.

"Four chocolate milkshakes, please," Mack said to Claire.

"I'm sorry," said Claire. "I've only got three milkshakes."

"Then Emma can't have one," said Luke.

"Luke!" said Uncle Lee and Dad.

Ivy and Mack took Emma to the playground. Emma climbed up. They all climbed! But at the top...

"I can't get down!" said Emma.

Luke came out of the café.

"Emma! It's OK. Don't worry. I'm here," said Luke.

"I'm sorry, Emma," said Luke. "There aren't too many Emmas. There is only one. And she is kind and fantastic. You are the best sister."

"No. Ivy is the best sister!" said Mack.

At the bus stop, Ivy looked at Luke and laughed. "Luke! Where's your swimming bag?"

Luke and Dad ran very fast to get his bag from the café.

"Has *everyone* got their bags now?" said Uncle Lee.

"Let's go home and make some milkshakes!" said Dad.

Picture dictionary

Listen and repeat

bus stop

bookshop

café

hospital

supermarket

swimming pool

1 Look and order the story

2 Listen and say

Collins

Published by Collins
An imprint of HarperCollins*Publishers*
Westerhill Road
Bishopbriggs
Glasgow
G64 2QT

HarperCollins*Publishers*
1st Floor, Watermarque Building
Ringsend Road
Dublin 4
Ireland

William Collins' dream of knowledge for all began with the publication of his first book in 1819.

A self-educated mill worker, he not only enriched millions of lives, but also founded a flourishing publishing house. Today, staying true to this spirit, Collins books are packed with inspiration, innovation and practical expertise. They place you at the centre of a world of possibility and give you exactly what you need to explore it.

© HarperCollins*Publishers* Limited 2020

10 9 8 7 6 5 4 3 2

ISBN 978-0-00-839808-8

Collins® and COBUILD® are registered trademarks of HarperCollins*Publishers* Limited

www.collins.co.uk/elt

British Library Cataloguing in Publication Data

A catalogue record for this publication is available from the British Library.

Author: Juliet Clare Bell
Lead illustrator: Gustavo Mazali (Beehive)
Copy illustrator: Szépvölgyi Eszter (Beehive)
Series editor: Rebecca Adlard
Publishing manager: Lisa Todd
Product managers: Jennifer Hall and Caroline Green
In-house editor: Alma Puts Keren
Project manager: Emily Hooton
Editor: Deborah Friedland
Proofreaders: Natalie Murray and Michael Lamb
Cover designer: Kevin Robbins
Typesetter: 2Hoots Publishing Services Ltd
Audio produced by id audio, London
Reading guide author: Julie Penn
Production controller: Rachel Weaver
Printed and bound by: GPS Group, Slovenia

Download the audio for this book and a reading guide for parents and teachers at www.collins.co.uk/839808